The Beginner's Bible

T0190621

Come Celebrate Easter

Sticker & Activity Book

ZONDERkidz

Copyright © 2015 by Zonderkidz
Zonderkidz, Grand Rapids, Michigan 49546

Illustrations: Denis Alonso
Design: Jody Langley

Printed in Malaysia

23 24 25 26 27 28 /RRDA/ 15 14 13 12 11 10

Color the people.

The Son of God

Jesus was the Son of God. He traveled all over Israel healing the sick and teaching people about God's amazing love.

Color Jesus.

Hosanna!

Many people loved Jesus. When Jesus went to Jerusalem, a big crowd welcomed him. People waved palm branches and put them on the road in front of Jesus. They shouted, "Hosanna! Hosanna! Blessed is the King of Israel!"

Use the stickers. Put palm branches in people's hands and on the road.

What kind of animal did Jesus ride into Jerusalem? Color the animal.

3

Jesus Is Betrayed

Not everyone loved Jesus. Some people wanted to hurt him because they were jealous. They made a plan to get rid of Jesus.

Find the stickers to complete the picture of Judas and the Jewish leaders.

Do you remember how many pieces of silver the leaders paid Judas to help get Jesus? Trace the number.

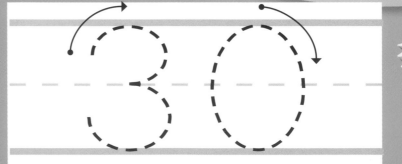

The Garden of Gethsemane

Jesus went to a garden to pray. The disciples came too. Jesus prayed, "I will do what you want, God. I am ready to give my life to save people from their sins."

How many stars can you count?____

How many flowers?____

Taken!

When Judas brought soldiers to the garden to arrest Jesus, all the disciples ran away.

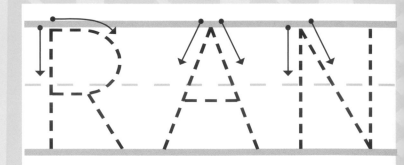

Practice writing RAN.

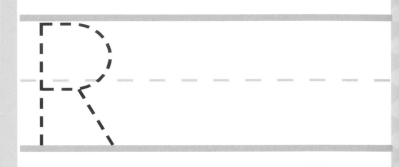

Circle the words that rhyme with **RAN.**

MAN

FISH

PLAN

DOG

Not the Son?

The soldiers took Jesus to the church leaders. They said, "You say that you are the Son of God. We do not believe you."

Can you spot the differences between these two pictures? There are 5. Circle the differences.

Because the disciples ran away, Jesus was all alone. Have you ever felt all alone?

_____.

Carrying the Cross

The soldiers took charge of Jesus. They made him carry a big wooden cross. They took him to a place called the Skull. They nailed Jesus to the cross. Jesus died.

Look at the pictures. Write the number 1 below what happened first. Write the number 2 below what happened second. Write the number 3 below what happened third. Write the number 4 below what happened last.

Can you find these words in the word search? Circle the words.

Christ
Cross
Easter
God
Jesus
Pray

V	C	H	R	I	S	T
Q	F	L	K	G	O	D
S	C	R	O	S	S	P
C	E	A	S	T	E	R
J	E	S	U	S	P	A
B	K	B	E	W	I	Y
G	C	G	Z	V	O	D

Color the people. Use stickers to complete the picture.

A Very Sad Day

Everyone who loved Jesus was very sad that he died. But they forgot something important. Jesus said he would see them again soon!

? What do you look like when you are sad? Draw a picture here.

Use stickers to add soldiers.

The tomb was in a garden. Use stickers to add flowers and plants.

In the Tomb

After Jesus died, some of his friends placed his body in a big tomb. It was sealed shut with a large round stone. Soldiers guarded the tomb.

The Third Day

Three days later, the earth shook. An angel of the Lord came down from heaven and pushed the stone away from the tomb. When the soldiers saw the angel, they fell to the ground.

Connect the dots around the angel.

Do you think the soldiers were afraid?
Yes____   No____

Not Here?

Mary was walking to the tomb with some of her friends. They saw the angel. The angel said, "Do not be afraid. Jesus is not here."

What else did the angel say?

Use the code to find out what the angel said to Mary and her friends!

Key Code

 = S

 = N

 = I

 = H

 = R

 = E

H _

I _

_ _ _ _ _ !

Start

Jesus Is Alive!

On their way out of the garden, the women saw Jesus. They fell to their knees and worshiped him. Jesus smiled and said, "Go tell the others that I will see them in Galilee." Run with Mary to tell the others!

Together Again

The disciples locked themselves in a small room. They were afraid the church leaders would send soldiers to arrest them. Suddenly, Jesus appeared! The disciples were so happy!

Add stickers to complete the picture.

Jesus said to the disciples, "Touch my hands and my feet so that you will know it is really me."

Put an X on the places where Jesus was hurt by nails.

Empty Nets

Later, the disciples went fishing. They fished all night, but did not catch even one fish. Early the next morning, someone from the shore shouted, "Cast your net on the other side of the boat." As soon as they did, their net was full of fish! Then the disciples knew the man was Jesus. Peter jumped out of the boat. He swam to shore.

Use stickers to add fish to fill the disciples' net.

Trace JESUS' name.

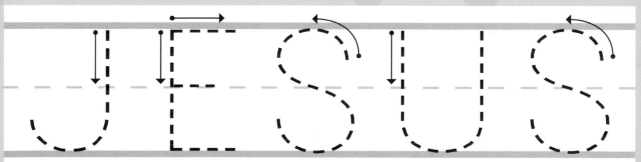

Jesus' Return to Heaven

The time came for Jesus to go back to heaven. But one day he will return.

Color-By-Number

0 = White
1 = Yellow
2 = Red
3 = Blue
4 = Green
5 = Purple
6 = Brown
7 = Orange